SHINING STAR

A SHORT STORY

ALEXANDRIA BLAELOCK

BlueMere Books
MELBOURNE, AUSTRALIA

For permission requests, please contact
enquiries@bluemerebooks.com.

Ordering Information:
Discounts are available on quantity purchases. For details, contact orders@bluemerebooks.com.

Shining Star/Alexandria Blaelock
paperback ISBN: 978-0-6481733-3-5
digital ISBN: 978-0-6481733-4-2

Book Layout © BookDesignTemplates.com

BlueMere Books
www.bluemerebooks.com

SHINING STAR

"**A**nd this is Jason Winter who'll be playing the male lead General Chang."

I'll be honest.

I hadn't been paying attention.

I'm the author of best-selling novel *Bayside Bloodshed*, and it's being made into a movie.

Yay me!

We authors can be a bit precious about our books, so we aren't usually invited to any cast or crew meetings.

I should have been more grateful and involved, but the Director had said something about a local archaeological dig, and it set my train of thought heading to a different station.

Could I send my hero General Chang to the pyramids?

I was staring out the window at a morning sky so blue and sunny I could almost smell the gum trees and nibbling at some kind of sweet pastry as I tried to work through how I'd get him there.

And what he might do when he got there.

I was slightly annoyed when my train got derailed.

Schooling my face into a polite smile, I turned to greet the star and gasped as I looked up at the General himself.

I mean really, Jason was exactly what I'd imagined as I wrote Chang.

Dark eyes with ridiculously long lashes, dark hair, clean-shaven, lovely long pointy sideburns.

Tight t-shirt revealing just enough lean muscle in all the right places.

What was worse, he smiled Chang's sardonic smile, seeming to understand my shock and surprise.

As if it happened *all* the time.

My stomach lurched, and for an instant, I thought I might throw up on him.

He held out his hand to shake.

I transferred the pastry to my left hand, wiped my sticky right one down the leg of my jeans and offered it to him.

His hand was warm and soft as it enfolded mine. He smelled of sandalwood soap.

Just like Chang.

Did he do it deliberately?

"Ms Mason," he said in a rich baritone, bowing his head a little, "pleased to meet you.

"I haven't read your book, but I've heard it's good. I'm looking forward to bringing Chang to life".

I swallowed.

So far as I could tell, he was doing an excellent job so far, but he was making me very uncomfortable.

And he didn't seem in any hurry to let my hand go.

Which was fantastic!

But I was starting to hyperventilate and didn't think passing out at his feet would be a good look.

I had to get away.

At last my Celebrity Author Persona clicked into place, "I'm sure you'll do well Mr Winter, I look forward to seeing your interpretation."

I tried to pull my hand back, but he held it firmly, pinning me in place with his gaze.

Like an ugly moth mounted on a dusty museum board in an antique cupboard.

He was going to make one hell of a General Chang.

Fortunately, the Director forced him to let me go by introducing me to the female lead - the Poor Girl didn't stand a chance against Chang.

I said something suitably encouraging (at least I hope so).

I'm often at functions making inane small talk with readers, but not usually with my back to a long streak of gorgeousness.

Thankfully it was soon time to leave the actors to their first rehearsal, and the Director handed me over to the Producer to introduce me to the crew.

I couldn't help myself but look back as I walked through the door, and Chang, I mean Winter, was smiling slightly as he watched me leave.

I tripped over my feet as I exited stage left.

So.

Not.

Cool.

The Producer, it turned out, had read the book. In fact, he loved it so much he was probably the reason it was now going into production.

I left my foolish starstruck writer in the corridor, firmly buttoned Celebrity Author Persona up to my chin, and set myself to charming the pants off him and the crew.

I signed copies of the book and told them a little about how the idea came to me, and the story grew.

We walked around the half-constructed sound stage, and they explained how the sets and rigs would be put together.

It was fun, and really much more interesting than I expected.

I asked lots of questions because you never know when some of this stuff might come in handy for a story.

And I had heaps of fun trying out some of the rigging.

I got the impression that a lot of people are more interested in the actors than the behind the scenes stuff, but when you think about it, you can't get much more behind the scenes than the writing.

These were more my people than the actors.

Several dirty but happy hours passed before I got the sense that it was time to leave, I wanted to play a bit longer, but it's always better to go out on a high.

The Producer escorted me to the main entrance and called for a car to take me back to my hotel.

I meant it sincerely when I thanked him for an exciting day and assured him I was fine to wait on my own.

I sprawled comfortably in a seat outside the empty reception room, legs outstretched, hands folded across my stomach, head leaning back.

My face was towards the sun, and I closed my eyes and took a deep breath of river scented air.

There was a lot to think about, and I wanted to re-board the Chang goes to Egypt train of thought before it left for good.

Not to mention enjoy some fresh air, and quiet time alone to recover from the day's event.

It's not a coincidence that writers are introverts.

But, no such luck.

The car that pulled up next to me was driven by none other than Jason Winter.

Who crawled out of the tiny red vintage E-type Jaguar convertible.

The same car I gave Chang.

"I'm heading in your direction, can I give you a lift?"

I really didn't want any more to do with Chang just then.

Five minutes on top of the months I'd spent in the visceral act of creating him was already too much for one lifetime.

I know that sounds contradictory given I was already thinking about his next adventure.

But in my defence, that was more along the lines of sending him out for groceries than sitting in a tiny space that was already too small to contain his essence, let alone me as well.

Might as well sit next to a time bomb waiting for it to go off.

"No thanks, a car's been ordered for me."

He leaned back against the front wing, crossing his legs and hooking his thumbs in his pockets.

"Well, actually, it hasn't. I overheard the order and cancelled it."

How rude!

"You'll be waiting a while if you don't come with me."

He drew on the ground with his toe and looked at me from lowered eyes in a head turned slightly away from me.

Classic Princess move.

It seemed I had no choice but to get into his absurdly tiny car.

Could I keep it professional?

He'd already seen me in my usual shambolically absent-minded writer guise.

Worth a try.

I reengaged the Celebrity Author Persona as I stood to walk to the car.

He bolted upright and turned to open the door for me.

Even worse, he offered his hand to hold as I collapsed into the car.

"So, how was your tour Ms Mason?" he asked as we drove off, roof folded back, down the highway into the sunset.

My long dark hair streamed behind me, and my writer's soul rebelled at the cliché.

Not to mention trying to ignore the heat radiating from his body.

The way he tossed his head to flick the hair out of his eyes.

And how he leaned a little towards me when he glanced at me as he asked the question.

"Oh, I enjoyed it immensely."

I groaned inwardly. Did I really say that?

What the hell (aside from Chang) was wrong with me?

Was it time to get real and drop the Celebrity Author Persona?

"Look, I'm sorry I sound like an idiot Mr Winter. I just can't see you through Chang."

He opened his mouth and took a breath to speak, but nothing came out.

He glanced at me, frowned a little and tried again.

Still nothing

"Do you know, I really don't know what to say to that."

"I guess there isn't anything you can say. It's like I've got you mixed up with your twin. You'll probably always be Chang to me."

Oops.

He smiled Chang's mocking smile again, "Well, perhaps you could start by calling me Jason."

Distracted by the sunlight glancing off the fine hairs on his forearms, I said "and you can call me Amy."

Oh my god, I'd told him my real name, not my pen name.

I mean really, what was wrong with me?

"Amy." The sound poured from his lips like a lovely drink of peaty Laphroaig whisky, and I felt a spark of excitement leap deep inside me.

Not Chang, I reminded myself, but I'm not sure either of us had a chance against the charismatic character I'd created.

I'd never expected to actually meet the man who lived inside my head.

"Yes Jason?"

"I think I'm going to have to buy your book."

"Are you sure it won't taint your performance?" Curious writer engaged for the moment.

"Maybe it will give me added depth."

"Well, I suppose at least you'll have a better idea of what he's thinking."

I let the Celebrity Author Persona take the lead again.

My poor writer's brain was miles away, already imagining what it would be like to stand on the red carpet with him at the film's premiere.

Wearing high heels with something long and shiny, feeling his arm tighten around my waist as he told reporters how much he loved my work.

In his deep sexy voice.

In between adoring gazes.

"Sorry, what was that?" I'd lost track of the actual conversation again.

I had to get rid of him before I started muttering the imaginary one.

"I said we're here."

"Oh, thanks! Look, if you want to read the book, I've a copy in my room you can have."

Oh well done Amy, now you'll never get rid of him.

"That's okay, the studio gave me one, I just didn't bother reading it."

Ouch!

I climbed out of the car, "Ah, Okay. Well, thanks for the ride Jason. Perhaps we'll meet again once day."

And I fled, like a coward, before I could let anything else slip.

Or him say anything for that matter.

Safely inside my overly luxurious production funded hotel suite, I poured myself a whisky (so I could drink the sound of his voice) and fired up my laptop.

Who exactly was this Jason Winter?

Well, it seemed he was famous.

Not that I should have been surprised about that.

He'd made a few critically acclaimed and highly popular action films, been nominated for a couple of awards and won one.

Was regularly seen about town with any number of pretty starlets.

(Why are they called starlets anyway, is it because despite appearances they're still babies?)

He was a couple of years younger than me, and grew up on a dairy farm in a country town.

He'd modelled a bit for pocket money at Agricultural College, and been "discovered" shooting a commercial for jeans.

He liked to go back to the farm periodically to "get back to his roots." He occasionally sang with his younger brother's band (who I had actually heard of and was a bit of a fangirl).

His favourite colour was blue, he had a cat, and he loved jam doughnuts.

Fascinating how much you can find out about someone on the net.

Whether any of it's true or not is another matter. After all, I'd been so disturbed about some of the things said about me that I'd given up googling myself and shut down all my Celebrity Author social media accounts.

I was tempted to check myself out for comparison, but a writer who wants to stay more or less sane never reads her reviews.

Instead, I poured myself another whisky and took it to the balcony door.

The city lights below me were bright enough to dim the stars above, and neon reflections flashed across the ceiling in a bright rainbow of colour.

I opened the door and walked out.

Setting my drink on the wrought iron table, I sat on one companion chair propping my feet on the other and listened to the sound of the night.

Seagulls squawking, people talking, car horns tooting on the street, fun and laughter in the hotel bar below.

My stomach grumbled. The complementary fruit basket wasn't what I was hungry for, so I grabbed my handbag and headed out.

We'd passed a noodle shop on the way back, and I had a sudden urge for spicy noodle soup.

But who should I meet as the elevator doors opened, but Jason Winter with a bag of something that smelled delicious.

"Amy! We meet again!"

I clutched my bag to my chest for protection, "Hello Jason, I was just on my way out."

"It's been a long day, and I thought you might be hungry."

"That's so sweet, but I'm off to see some local friends before I fly home tomorrow."

I'm a writer, I can lie with the best of them.

"Oh. Well, I wanted to apologise. I thought you might be offended when I dismissed your book offer."

"Well, um, thank you. That's very kind.

He jiggled the food bag, "Are you sure you have to go out?"

Time stood still for a moment as I stood drowning in his eyes.

Why not indulge the fantasy? It's not like I would ever see him (or Chang) again.

If I needed an excuse, I'd call it in-depth research.

Goodbye caution, have a good time with the wind.

"Okay, sure. It was more of an "if you're not busy" thing anyway."

I led him back down the corridor, acutely aware that he was following only a step or two behind, and trying not to sway my hips too provocatively.

I'm not sure I was successful.

Letting him in was a mistake.

As large as the suite was, he seemed to take up entirely too much of it, sucking all the oxygen out of it.

Even though I'd accidentally left the balcony door open.

Even though it was a bigger space than the car I'd recently escaped from.

The air was thick with seething untold stories and his sandalwood scent inescapable.

How could it be more intense now than when I first met him, what eight, ten hours ago?

I could hear ghostly echoes of him calling out my name in the throes of passion.

Hey wait a minute.

Who was calling my name?

Was it Jason, or was it Chang?

Did it matter?

Trying to pretend everything was fine, and that I wasn't living multiple lives simultaneously, I static-shocked us both as I brushed past him on my way back to the mini-bar.

And kicked my shoes off, hoping the smell of my feet wasn't stronger than his soap.

He said, "I didn't know what you'd like so I got noodle soup - plain or spicy, and all the sides. I hope that's ok."

Had I slipped into a parallel universe?

"I was just thinking about spicy noodle soup. Would you like to share?"

"Yes please, that one's my favourite."

He took a seat, started pulling food out of the bag and arranging it on the table.

I crouched inelegantly to pull a bottle of Sauvignon Blanc from the fridge (phew, feet fine) and brought it to the table with a couple of chilled glasses and a corkscrew.

He took the lids off the food containers, while I poured the wine.

After a short interlude of reason trying to reassert itself, I ignored it and sat in the chair next to him.

All the better to eat soup with.

I had this one night to live the life of one of my characters.

Tomorrow I'd be back at home, in my daggy track pants, accompanied only by my farty geriatric dog and overly vivid imagination.

This trip would fade to a dream, and I'd probably never see Jason Winter again, well not unless I watched the film.

And while I had a creative veto, I'm not sure I could sit through the result anyway.

Your critical voice can be a real killer.

He tapped a pack of chopsticks on the table to break it open, then handed it to me.

I watched him open his, his movements graceful and economical.

I wondered if he'd taken martial arts or dance classes as a child. Or was it just the result of chasing cows in the clean country air.

Right up until my fifth book sales went nuts, I'd been a City girl, so I had no idea.

I cut myself off as I started to imagine a romantic life on a farm with him.

That was a step too far.

I must have made some kind of vocalisation (not uncommon for a woman who lives alone, let alone one who writes) and he raised one eyebrow at me.

"Sorry, occupational hazard. When you're a writer, you're never really in touch with reality.

"And you're almost always talking to imaginary friends."

Wow, I'd really let reason go.

But it was so nice to not have to pretend to be Someone Else for a moment.

And they say it's easier to talk to strangers than friends.

"What about you. What's your life like when you're not acting?"

I picked up some noodles and slurped them as he thought about his answer.

"I suppose it's the opposite. People don't see me, they confuse me with the characters I play."

"Ouch! Touché."

He exhaled a laugh as he picked up some noodles too, "It's an interesting change to be confused with a character before I play him."

I couldn't help laughing. "Is that why you go home? So the people you grew up with can remind you who you are?"

Oops, sprung! He'd know I'd Googled him now.

"Exactly so."

He caught my chopsticks in his. I'm not sure whether he meant to, but when I looked up at him, he was studying me intently.

My first thought was that I had soup on my face, so I wiped my lips with the back of my hand.

His eyes darted to my lips and back up again. I was looking at his lips as he reflexively licked them.

As helpless as a moth drawn to a flame, I couldn't stop myself leaning forward to kiss him. His soup flavoured lips were soft and warm.

As I started to pull away, he dropped his sticks and reached out with both hands to pull me back, kissing me deeply, passionately.

I was a little confused. I knew why I wanted him, well not Jason exactly, but I couldn't fathom what he wanted from me given we'd not spent more than about half an hour together.

That pesky reasoning part of me started up again, but I was committed to living this story now, if only for a short time, so I shut it down before it really got going.

He pulled away and looked at me closely.

Tentatively, he reached and undid one of my shirt buttons, and I wished I'd worn something with a lower neckline.

I think he was looking for some sign of rejection, and when it didn't come, he undid another button.

And then another, and smoothed his fingertips across my décolletage.

Which tingled so deliciously I gasped and shut my eyes.

It had been such a long time since a hand other than mine had been so intimate.

Did he feel the same sense of something missing?

His light touch was enough.

I dropped my chopsticks and went for his t-shirt, trying to get it over his head, but only succeeding in getting it caught on his ears.

He sort of shouldered me aside and stood to pull it off himself.

His hairless tanned chest was even more spectacular than I'd imagined.

I slowly reached up and gently placed my palm above his heart, and his muscles twitched.

As I looked up at him, he covered my hand with his and leaned down to kiss me again.

Ah yes, that was it.

I started tugging at my buttons and managed to get my shirt off.

I only avoided falling off the chair because he pulled me to my feet.

Still kissing me as he expertly undid my bra.

Oops, reason nearly got its foot in the door there.

Intoxicated once more by the scent of sandalwood, I ran my hands up his smooth chest and across the back of his shoulders holding him to my naked chest.

As he tried to straighten up, I wrapped my legs around his waist. He took a ragged breath and looked at me again.

"That way," I said waving a hand in the direction of the bedroom and gently bit his neck where the vein pulsed.

And at that point dear reader, we'll leave it there and imagine the swell of music, fireworks and waves crashing to the shore.

It was all that and more, but there are some things a girl has to treasure for herself and not dilute by sharing.

I hadn't expected Jason to still be there in the morning; Chang would've left during the night.

I was embarrassed, I didn't want Jason to know that I hadn't slept with him, and in the cold light of day, I wasn't sure that I wanted to have sex with him either.

Not to mention that I was a little hungover. And didn't want him to think I was just another fangirl.

My carry-on bag was already packed and waiting by the main suite door. I darted around the bedroom picking up my clothes, abandoning my toiletries and carefully tiptoeing out of the bedroom, quietly shutting the door behind me.

I dressed quickly, but not really quietly, and raced around the room collecting my laptop and handbag.

I was just about to exit stage right when I remembered I'd offered him a copy of the book.

I collapsed on a chair at the table for a moment, narrowly missing a bowl of cold soup, while I thought it through.

Should I just leave it?

Or should I write something in it?

Which name should I sign - true or pen?

Would he find it and take it, or would he leave it for the maid?

What would a Celebrity Author who'd had a one-night stand with the actor playing her hero do?

What would a woman who'd had the best sex in her sad, solitary life do?

I took the dog-eared copy I'd been using to refresh my memory with from my bag, shoved the half-eaten soup aside and using my trademark archival-quality purple ink pen (got to think of the fans) simply wrote

Thanks,

Amy

x

And then tiptoed back into the bedroom and left it on the bed next to him.

And exited quietly, stage left.

I had a plane to catch.

I thought of him many times over the next few months, and now and again I'd see him on the news with some pretty lady or other.

I didn't hear from him, so it seemed he was satisfied with the outcome of our night together.

In my more generous moments, I gave him the benefit of the doubt - he didn't know my true name.

But in less generous moments, I thought he might have at least tried. Others had found me with seemingly little difficulty.

But who was I kidding?

If I didn't know who I'd slept with, how could he? And it still wasn't clear why he'd slept with me.

Was he maybe doing his own research?

But there was no doubt our night together had inspired me.

I'd started writing almost before the plane had taken off, and General Chang's Egyptian Adventure was ready and waiting by the time my publisher asked for it.

How ironic that they'd waited so long to ask for a book to release at the same time as the movie.

At least they were prepared to rush it into print.

I'd written a charmingly cryptic dedication Jason would understand if he happened to see it.

And should he happen to read it, he'd probably recognise that I'd written what I knew.

Though I didn't know what he might think about that.

I hadn't heard a whisper about our brief interlude, or read any gossip about it.

While I was happy to avoid the speculation, I was still jealous of the pretty ladies.

I was surprised when my publisher called to let me know they were working together with the studio on a joint book and film promotion.

The studio would be making all the arrangements and would contact me in due course.

Book tours are always exhausting. Too much travel in too short a time, and too many people making too much noise.

It looked as though this would be a biggie - Jason's last movie had been a sell-out success, and he was now the hottest "new" star on the scene.

By the time my plane landed (in the middle of the night), I'd worked myself into a frenzy over what might happen.

With Jason, with the press, the movie, the book, the premiere.

I was so tense I thought I might snap!

I mentioned my vivid writer's imagination, right?

The horrors I'd imagined were nothing compared to what I walked into - cameras flashing, reporters calling out to me, people screaming.

It's not what I'm used to, and I thought the studio could have warned me.

I was very grateful the studio chauffeur was near enough to grab me and whisk me away in next to no time.

Though I suppose he was trained to wait just long enough for good exposure and no more.

I was also grateful I'd had the foresight to change my clothes, comb my hair and put on some lipstick before leaving border control.

Especially a couple of hours later when I saw my photo splashed across the morning papers.

JESSICA MASON AUTHOR
OF GENERAL CHANG
MYSTERIES ARRIVES FOR
FILM PREMIERE.

I hadn't even had breakfast, and my book tour was off with a bang.

As was my studio assigned stylist.

I swear she did not stop talking the entire time she was measuring me, waving clothes at me to see what suited, and checking to see if I liked it.

She more or less kicked aside my poor travel bag as she hung my new studio approved wardrobe. Thankfully not too vampish, though perhaps slightly more librarian in style than my usual choices.

Howls of laugher - as if I'd chosen a style!

I'd be on morning TV within a couple of hours. So the stylist sent me to bathe and wash my hair while she ordered coffee and breakfast, and liaised with the hair and makeup artists.

When I came out, they rushed to style me and sent me back to the car with gift copies of the new Chang mystery (Jason's face prominently on the cover) for the hosts.

My assigned assistant gabbled at me about pitches and gifts for studio audiences and led me into a waiting room.

Which I paced up and down, summoning inner peace while waiting for my turn under the lights.

And then I was being hustled on set to explain where the stories came from. And how I felt about the film and what I thought about the Director and actors.

And off into the car for a change of clothes and a mid-morning show.

Then back to the car for a change of clothes and taping a spot for the evening news.

I didn't know it at the time, but there was a set of rooms like stables.

I sat in one, the Director in another, Jason and the female lead in a third, and some other people in yet other rooms. The reporters funnelled through, ten minutes with each of us to be edited to fit their needs.

He was right next door all along, and I had no idea. I'm amazed I couldn't feel his energy through the walls.

As my last reporter left and my gaggle of studio lackeys descended upon me through the open door, I caught sight of him walking down the corridor with his lackeys clamouring for his attention.

He gave me a tight smile as he strode past my door, neither pausing nor otherwise giving any indication of intimacy.

Just.

That.

Cold.

I couldn't tell if he was busy, discreet or just plain didn't care about me.

I felt myself slump as the scent of sandalwood in his wake hit me and dashed my unarticulated hopes.

But, I was there to do a job, so I squared my shoulders, straightened my spine and put on my Celebrity Author Persona.

I smiled at bookshop signings, performed readings, gracefully accepted the compliments of daytime TV, and laughed at inane Chang jokes.

Even Author events can be solitary and lonely events.

At the end of each day, I was so grateful to be back in the quiet stillness of my room that its empty storylessness didn't really bother me.

I ate room service and watched him on night time chat shows spruiking the movie.

He was charming, self-deprecating and amusing, relating stories about on set hijinks and praising the Director and his co-stars.

Not a word about me, though realistically, why would there be?

How does that Nat King Cole song go? Smiling, heart breaking, aching, whatever it is.

Naturally, the two clips they used were:

a.   the climactic choreographed fight scene, and

b.   the one where he steps out of the dark to swoop the damsel in distress up in his arms with a passionate kiss.

I could almost imagine his friends and family laughing at him and keeping his ego manageable.

How I wanted to be there with them rather than here in this celebrity merry-go-round.

The grim humour of being jealous of people I hadn't met was not lost on me.

How exactly had I come to this place of loneliness?

Damn you writer's imagination!

Finally, the night of the premier arrived, and I wasn't sure how I felt.

The clever studio stylist arrived before I had a chance to chicken out and refuse to go.

I hadn't forgotten my red-carpet story, and the stunning deep red bias-cut dress she offered was a powerful incentive.

It was elegant in its simplicity, with a demure high neckline, tight long sleeves and a full yet flat skirt.

We'll just gloss over how difficult it was to get into the foundation garments required for a smooth silhouette in a fitted dress. And how long it took to do up all the tiny pearl buttons down the back.

The hairstylist swept my hair up into a tall braided coronet.

Then it was time for makeup, again understated, and a spritz of some kind of madly sophisticated sexy musky fragrance.

Wicked Witch of the East ruby slippers, red clutch, diamond earrings, and an enormous diamond broach pinned to my left shoulder.

I was ready. Just in time for the chauffeur.

Now, I'm what they like to call petite.

In fact, I'm smaller than petite, but I felt as tall and glamorously beautiful as the best of them as I lifted my skirt Disney Princess style and started down the grand staircase.

How fortunate I'd taken some deportment classes for research and could descend stairs without looking at them.

I can't tell you how satisfied I was to find a throng of photographers waiting at the bottom.

I've no idea whether they were waiting for me, but I leaned nonchalantly on the bannister, posing prettily while I surreptitiously looked for my driver.

Nor can I say how surprised I was when Jason, still sporting Chang's hair and pencil moustache, appeared from the shadows.

He took my hand and brought it to his lips, then tucked it through his arm. "You look beautiful," he said.

"You're not too shabby yourself."

He looked gorgeous in a slim tuxedo, with his hair casually swept back from his face.

Unusually for a premiere, he wore a fresh red rose in his lapel. One that matched the colour of my dress exactly.

Clever studio stylist.

We stood for a moment before he bowed his head to the photographers and led me towards the exit.

Oh.

My.

God.

Not only was I a Princess for a few hours, but Jason Winter was my Prince Charming.

I'm so amazed I didn't trip or fall, my knees felt so weak!

Safely in the relative privacy of a dark windowed limousine, and enveloped in an intoxicating warm cloud of sandalwood, he kissed me.

Deeply.

Thoroughly.

Mintily.

I'm not sure about my lipstick, but when he was done, there was not one hair out of place on my head.

Which was swimming.

Do movie stars go to classes to learn how to kiss without messing up hair?

I'd have to look into that.

He cradled the back of my neck in his right hand, forcing me to meet his gaze, while gently caressing the edge of my chin with his thumb.

"I promise you, the next time we're together, you'll know you're sleeping with me, and not him."

And then he kissed me again.

My insides turned to jelly, and reason left me without a word to say in reply.

I wanted that so bad.

Right then and there would have been perfectly fine.

It seemed we arrived at the theatre in no time at all.

The chauffeur opened the door for Jason, who he got out, then held out his hand to help me out of the car.

As I placed my hand in his, he bent to kiss it, and the photographers went nuts.

What was it with this guy and the hand kissing? Though, I kinda liked it.

My deportment lessons covered how to exit a car like a lady too, so all good there.

We stood, still holding hands as cameras flashed all around us. He looked down at me and smiled, which naturally made me smile back, and the photographers redoubled their efforts to get the perfect shot.

As the next car pulled in, he turned and led me up the stairs and into the dimly lit theatre.

Still holding my hand, which now trembled a little, he took me from group to group of actors and film industry people.

I *really* tried not to act like too much of a fangirl. And to be gracious when they said they loved my books.

Celebrity Author Persona had abandoned me, and in any case, it always makes me feel weird when someone compliments my work.

Soon enough, it was time to take a seat and watch the movie.

Movie Chang was edgier than mine; his movements more dynamic, and his attitude more aggressive.

I didn't really like this Chang, but there was no doubt he was magnetic.

Now and again I'd look over at the man whose fingers were entwined in mine.

As if sensing my confusion, he'd give me a small smile and squeeze my hand or smooth his thumb across the back of it.

And the audience would laugh, and I'd look up at him on the big screen again.

I mean I already knew he was not my Chang, let alone the hard man on the screen, but I didn't know who he was.

As screen Chang kissed Poor Girl and started taking her clothes off, I closed my eyes, so I didn't have to watch.

And as the light flickered through my closed lids, I wondered what his mother thought of his on-screen intimacies.

Yes, I was jealous - Poor Girl was doing a better job than I'd expected.

I wondered if his mother had met any of his co-stars.

And I wondered what she'd think of me.

All too soon the credits rolled, and the red velvet curtain closed.

The audience called for the Director who took to the stage and made a short speech praising the crew before calling Jason and his co-star on stage. They made their own speeches, but I wasn't listening.

My writing brain had kicked in, and I was thinking about a disaster at a movie premiere. How flammable were the furnishings, and what kind of fire retardant would they deploy and how long it would take to put the fire out.

I lost the plot when the sound of thunderous applause hit and a spotlight suddenly shone in my face.

"Ladies and Gentlemen," the Director announced, "I'd like to introduce you to the author of the General Chang books, Ms Jessica Mason. Please come on up Jessica."

I should have been paying attention.

Hopefully, he'd have explained what he wanted by the time I got up to the stage.

Fixing my eyes on Jason, I descended the stairs.

As I approached the stage, he came to meet me. Taking my hand, he bent to kiss my cheek and quietly asked, "Did you see enough of the movie to say something nice?"

I dipped my head in ascent and allowed him to escort me to the microphone.

I looked out over a sea of famous faces as the applause died down.

Turning to the audience on my right, I started with "Wow", and turning to the left, I shrugged my shoulder "I mean, just Wow."

Looking to the front, I fanned myself with an imaginary fan, "Ho boy, that was some movie."

A smattering of laughter.

I turned to smile at the Director, Poor Girl and Jason, "I think you've ruined the books for me."

The audience laughed, and applause broke out as I backed away from the microphone.

I'd planned to sidle behind the group, but Jason put his arm around my waist and pulled me back to stand between him and the Director as the photographers started up again.

No wonder he had to escape it all now and again.

It seemed to last forever, but I suppose it wasn't much more than a minute before the Director led us off the stage.

And along yet another red carpet for quick sound bite interviews, waving and autograph signing.

I prefer the solitary writing side of being an author, and Jason thwarted each of my attempts to skip ahead and away from the attention.

Whether he took my hand, clasped my waist or clutched my shoulder, there was no getting away from his touch.

The heat of his hands seared through my clothes, constantly reminding me of his promise.

Though I had no idea how he was going to get me out of the corsetry.

I was on fire, and I had no choice but to squirm discreetly and go with the flow.

Thank god the stylist had chosen something pretty as well as practical.

Finally, we made it to the end of the carpet and into a limousine heading to the after-party.

Alone, aside from the driver who discretely closed the connecting window.

Jason pulled me into his lap, and I became aware that I wasn't the only one who wanted to move things forward.

There wasn't much bare skin he could access, but he reached under the skirt and ran his hands up my legs to clasp my buttocks as he kissed me again.

Too soon the driver's tinny voice came over the intercom to say we were pulling into the hotel.

I slid off his lap and smoothed my skirt, trying not to smile as he adjusted his trousers.

And when the car door opened, I was ecstatic to find we were back at my hotel.

Sadly, no sneaking off just yet though, more photographers, and through to a big party of movie star peers to celebrate the end of the project.

Jason loosened his tie as he led me across to a love seat in a small alcove.

He sat and pulled me down next to him, one hand casually resting on my thigh as he toyed with my fingers with the other.

Clearing his throat, he looked at me, "I read your book."

"How nice. Which one?"

"The new one, the one you wrote for me."

I couldn't help myself, "did you buy it, or did the studio give it to you?"

He sighed, and I regretted the words immediately.

"I suppose I deserved that. I don't know where the book came from, I assumed you. Though now that I think about it, it was unsigned and came to my real name."

Ooh, you've got to love a good mystery, haven't you?

"I was angry when I woke and you'd gone. I couldn't believe you'd left me as if nothing had happened."

It was my turn to be ashamed. I opened my mouth to reply, but he pressed an index finger against my lips to stop me.

I resisted the temptation to lick it.

"You didn't seem to have any idea who I was, and we shared a strong attraction, so I thought we'd made a genuine connection. That despite what you said, you could see me through Chang and Jason. I don't know who I was more jealous of.

"And then I found this," he pulled aside his collar to reveal my every day chakra necklace."

So that's where it went.

"There hasn't been a day gone by that I haven't worn this and thought of you. I need to be with you, but I have no idea who you are."

I couldn't stand it any longer, I licked his finger.

His eyes darkened, and with a groan, he took my face in both hands and kissed me.

I thought I could get used to that.

"Can we go now?" I asked when he let me go.

And maybe we would, if the Producer hadn't arrived with champagne and a couple of guys from the crew.

Despite the timing, I was really glad to see them.

Blushing furiously, I patted Jason's leg and stood to talk to them. He stood too, and after a round of handshaking and congratulations, he said "I'll catch you later," and disappeared into the crowd.

I accepted some good-natured ribbing about Jason and followed the guys to chat with the rest of the crew.

Who introduced me to other people, and now and again, someone wanted to meet Jessica Mason.

Or the woman in red.

And all the while I was turning to see Jason looking back at me across the crowded room, though given my height that was nothing short of miraculous.

As the crowd started thinning out, he appeared behind me and snaked an arm around my waist.

It was time.

In an attempt to avoid detection, we left through a side door, skirted a utility area and took the service elevator.

Suddenly I was overcome with shyness and turned away from him.

"I thought of you too...

"I was afraid of what I might see in your eyes that morning. You're some hotshot movie star, and I'm just some daggy chick the studio flew in for the day.

"You probably have women throwing themselves at you every day - how can I compete with that?"

A tear rolled down my cheek as I took a ragged breath.

He kissed the nape of my neck, pulled me back against his chest and enclosed me in his arms.

"They don't see me like you do. I'm not even a person to them, something more like a scalp."

He dropped a kiss on the top of my head, then rested his chin on it. "We don't have to do anything you don't want to do. Now or ever."

Though a stray finger was idly drawing hot circles on my ribcage and it was almost more than I could bear.

Fortunately, the elevator binged to indicate our arrival at my floor.

I caught up my skirt in one hand, and grabbed his in the other and ran down the corridor.

I hoped that all those stylists had packed their bags and left.

And thank goodness they had.

Slamming the door behind us, ruby slippers on both feet, I leaned back against it and looked up at him.

He put his free hand on it for support and leaned down to kiss me, before crushing my body against his with the other.

I made a small sound, so he took my hand and led me to the bedroom where he started to unbutton the dress, dropping kisses down my spine as he went.

Every time I reached for him, he slapped my hand away.

Definitely not a Chang move.

Once the dress had fallen to the floor, I reached for him again, and he allowed me to do to the same for him while he pulled the pins from my hair and ran his fingers through it, smoothing it out across my shoulders.

Also not a Chang move.

And the next bit's private.

And the bit after that.

Then the next bit too.

Goodness me, let's just pick it up the next morning.

I lay on my side, one hand supporting my cheek and looked closely at him in the light.

He hadn't completely shaken Chang off; aside from the hair, there was still something dangerous about him.

I ran a finger lightly across the moustache and up his cheek to tuck his hair behind his ear, allowing my palm to cradle his cheek.

I wondered how long it took an actor to let a character go, or did the character become a part of them?

Did you just need to push the right button to bring them back to the surface?

Or was it like writing, where you left a piece of yourself behind forever?

He opened his eyes and looked at me for a moment before turning to kiss the palm of my hand.

"Coffee?" I asked.

He yawned and scrubbed his eyes, "Ah god, that would be wonderful."

I left him to make whatever morning preparations men need and set the espresso machine in motion.

Despite laying out two mugs, I forgot for a moment that he was there as I scratched my head, and combed my hair with my hands, dislodging a couple of hidden pins.

Eyes closed, standing on tip-toes I was stretching tall when his cool hands captured my breasts.

I'd forgotten I was naked too.

Laughing at my startled squeak, he offered me a robe.

We sat companionably drinking coffee, soaking up the warm sunshine on the balcony.

My feet rested in his lap, and he was idly stroking my leg under the robe.

It occurred to me that I still didn't know his true name.

"So, Mystery Man, if you're not General Chang or Jason Winter, what is your name?"

He took another sip of his coffee, and smiled enigmatically, "You tell me yours first."

Eyes rolled.

I held out my hand, "Amy Prescott."

He took it, turned it palm upwards and kissed it, "Hello Amy Prescott, my name is Song Kai. I'm very pleased to meet you."

"Kai." Oh, that was the perfect name.

"Kai, the pleasure is all mine."

THE END

ABOUT THE AUTHOR

Alexandria Blaelock writes stories, some of them for *Ellery Queen's Mystery Magazine* and *Pulphouse Fiction Magazine*. She's also written four self-help books applying business techniques to personal matters like getting dressed, cleaning house, and feeding your friends.

As a recovering Project Manager, she's probably too fond of sticking to plan. She lives in a forest because she enjoys birdsong, the scent of gum leaves and the sun on her face. When not telecommuting to parallel universes from her Melbourne based imagination, she watches K-dramas, talks to animals, and drinks Campari. At the same time.

Discover more at www.alexandriablaelock.com.

OTHER SHORT STORIES BY ALEXANDRIA BLAELOCK

Kiss of Death
Long Weekend in the Snow
Shining Star
Phoenix Child
Ship in a Bottle
Lady of the Looking Glass
Simone Says Hands in the Air
Life in the Security Directorate
Fate in Your Hands
Love in the Security Directorate
Alma's Grace
Payton's Run
The Guardian's Vigil
The Life and Death of Carmelita Basingstoke
Balancing the Book

BOOKS BY
ALEXANDRIA BLAELOCK

Stress Free Dinner Parties
Build Your Signature Wardrobe
Holistic Personal Finance
Ms Blaelock's Book of Minimally Viable
Housekeeping

www.ingramcontent.com/pod-product-compliance
Lightning Source LLC
Chambersburg PA
CBHW061926130726
47909CB00012B/1796